The MAGICAL MUSEUM

VILLAGE WHISPERS

WEAM NAMOU

HERMiZ
PUBLiSHING
Copyright © 2025 by Weam Namou

Library of Congress Cataloging-in-Publication Data
2025912480
Namou, Weam

The Magical Museum
Village Whispers
(Middle Grade Fiction)
ISBN
978-1-945371-16-5 (paperback)

978-1-945371-17-2 (eBook)

First Edition

Published in the United States of America by:
Hermiz Publishing, Inc.
Sterling Heights, MI

10 9 8 7 6 5 4 3 2 1

The MAGICAL MUSEUM

VILLAGE WHISPERS

CHAPTER 1

A Village in the Museum

As we stepped into the next room, it felt as though we had left the museum entirely and entered a world suspended in time. The scent of freshly baked bread drifted through the air, mingling with the faint earthy aroma of dried herbs hanging from wooden beams. The room was alive—vivid murals of rolling hills and stone houses stretched across the walls and the soft glow of lanterns painted the space in hues of amber and gold.

At the center of it all stood a tableau of village life: a Chaldean woman kneeling on the ground, rolling out dough for *lukhma d'rekki*—thin, crispy bread. She wore a long house dress with two neat braids draped over her shoulders and a headdress tied securely around her head. Her gold cross necklace glinted softly under the lantern light, and dangling earrings—not real gold, but close enough to fool a sixth grader—swung gently with her movements.

She greeted us with her eyes, and I greeted her in return.

"That's her!" a few children shouted, pointing at the woman. Others whispered, their voices filled with awe.

"She looks like my grandmother," Mary said, her tone humble as she adjusted her notebook.

"She looks like my grandmother *if* my grandmother baked bread in a museum," John said, gaining a high-five from Zaya.

"John!" his mother, Helen, the chaperone, warned, lowering her glasses with a sharp look. She then patted her red hair and pretty polka dot dress.

The woman's lifelike expression seemed to welcome us, as if she were about to offer freshly baked bread, a cup of chai, and a seat by the *soup*a (heater) or *tanoor* (clay oven). I could almost hear her say, "Come, eat, rest, and share your news," just as Chaldean women often did.

I adjusted my blazer and smoothed my long, straight hair. The gold necklace and bracelets from Baghdad jingled as I checked my phone for the time. I then stepped closer toward the group. "This gallery isn't just about artifacts or history; it's about stories. Every corner of this room holds a piece of the villages that shaped the Chaldean people—each one unique, yet part of a shared legacy."

Mr. Yatooma cleared his throat dramatically, his tall, slender figure stepping up beside me. "And do you know what makes this gallery so special, kids?" He paused, his moustache twitching with energy as his eyes sparkled.

"It has bread?" Zaya guessed.

"And gupta?" someone else chimed in.

"Baklava?" a child added, then giggled. Other words such as "Taghratha" and other popular food items were tossed around like hot potatoes, and the children got rowdy.

"Well, yes, but that's not the point," Mr. Yatooma interrupted with mock indignation. "This gallery is special because it shows us how our ancestors lived—how they survived and thrived in places like Tel Keppe, Bartella, Alqosh, and hundreds of other villages. Every tool, every piece of bread, every sack of burghul tells a story."

John held up a piece of grain and placed his ear beside it. "I don't hear anything, Mr. Yatooma."

The children roared with laughter while John eyed the grain. "Hey, got something to tell me?"

"John, stop that!" said Helen.

"Children, clam down," I said, and gestured toward a farm scene nearby. "Take a look over there."

They followed my direction.

In the corner, a small farm display stood out. A

man dressed in the traditional clothes of Tel Keppe worked in the fields, surrounded by sacks of burghul and other grains popular in Chaldean villages. Farming tools rested nearby, their wooden handles worn smooth from years of use. The man appeared to be preparing for a journey, his gaze fixed on the road ahead as if ready to sell his goods in neighboring villages.

"Can you guess which village this is?" I asked, pointing to a small diorama nestled in the corner. It was a miniature replica of a village, complete with stone houses, a church with a tall steeple, and a vineyard stretching toward the horizon.

"Tel Keppe?" Lola guessed, tilting her head.

Before I could reply, Zaya jumped in. "And let me guess, the man's about to walk ten miles uphill in both directions to sell burghul in another village—just like the stories my mom used to tell."

"Good guess," I said, nodding. "Tel Keppe—also called Telkaif—is one of the oldest and most important Chaldean villages. Well, technically, it's a town because it's larger and more significant than a typical village, but people still call it a village."

"Was it as famous as Buckingham Palace?" Lola asked dreamily.

I laughed. "Maybe not quite, but it was famous among Chaldeans. Its original name meant 'Hill of

Stones' in Chaldean, but as Arabic became more dominant in the region, it changed to Telkaif—or 'Hill of Joy.'"

Zaya raised an eyebrow. "Wait, so they just decided to make it sound happier?"

"That's one way to look at it," I said. "But the name change comes from the Arabic alphabet, which doesn't have the letter 'p,' so it was swapped for 'f.' The meaning changed a bit along the way."

"Stones to joy," Zaya murmured, shaking his head. "That's quite a makeover."

Mr. Yatooma cleared his throat, preparing for a speech. "Kids, Tel Keppe is more than just a hill of stones—or joy, for that matter. This town has a story that goes back thousands of years. The hill itself was likely built during the reign of the Akkadians, Assyrians, and Chaldeans. It was originally a lookout point to protect Nineveh, the capital of the Assyrian Empire."

He paused, raising a finger in the air. "A captain would stand on that hill, ready to light a fire to warn the city of approaching enemies. Other fortresses would catch the signal and pass it along like an ancient game of telephone."

"Or like sending a group text," John interrupted.

"Great comparison!" Mr. Yatooma exclaimed,

pointing at John like he'd solved a great mystery. "Except, instead of emojis, they used fire."

The group chuckled, and I jumped back in. "Over time, Tel Keppe became more than just a warning station. By the nineteenth century, people were using its hill as a cemetery. And during one burial in 1889, something incredible happened. A man digging a grave for his father uncovered a hidden well—cold, clear water that had been untouched for centuries."

"That's amazing," Mary said, her pencil hovering over her notebook.

"It is," I replied. "The well turned out to be part of an ancient system of canals built during the Assyrian Empire. Over the years, people uncovered more channels and even a statue in one of the wells. Some are still mysteries today."

"So, they were burying people on top of old water systems?" Lola asked, wide-eyed.

"Pretty much," I said. "And they didn't even know it until they started digging. But Tel Keppe's history isn't all hidden wells and happy name changes. The village has faced its share of hardships."

Mr. Yatooma picked up the thread with enthusiasm. "In the 1500s, Mongol invaders attacked Tel Keppe, and in the 1700s, Persian armies destroyed Christian villages around Mosul. Tel Keppe became a refuge for people fleeing these invasions. Over time, it turned into a melting pot of Chaldean culture, uniting families from all over Mesopotamia."

He paused, looking at the group. "Do you know what makes that special?"

Zaya raised his hand. "Is it the bread?"

"No!" Mr. Yatooma said. "It's the resilience. Despite invasions, locusts, famines—you name it—Tel Keppe's people rebuilt their homes, their churches, their lives. They didn't just survive; they thrived."

Mary scribbled furiously in her notebook. "So, Tel Keppe is basically the 'never give up' village?"

"You could say that," I began, hesitantly. "Its history was one of resilience and community until 2014."

"What happened in 2014?" she asked.

"Well, that's when the ISIS attacked the village and brought it to ruins," I said.

"ISIS?" someone asked.

"The Islamic State of Iraq and Syria," I explained.

"Was Tel Keppe completely destroyed?" Mary asked with a concerned expression.

"Sadly, it was," I said. "There's more about the invasions and hardships in the Genocide Gallery. For now, let's focus on the life they preserved."

I gestured to a display showing a farmer tending his crops, a simple wooden plow beside him. "My grandparents were farmers," I began. "Like many in their village, their lives revolved around the land. They'd wake up at dawn to work the fields, go to church—sometimes *twice* a day—and spend the evenings with family, sharing meals and drinking chai. They had no electricity, which meant no iPad, TVs, or even phones!"

The kids gasped in unison.

"How did they *survive*?" Zaya asked, throwing his hands up in disbelief.

"Well," I said, "they got really good at talking to each other. You know, *face-to-face*. They'd sit together over chai or a meal and actually *listen*. Can you imagine?"

The kids giggled, some glancing at each other as though trying to picture it.

"Life was simple, but it was full," I said. "There were no TikToks, but they had stories, songs, and each other."

The kids turned back to the display, their earlier shock giving way to curiosity.

"Okay," Zaya said after a moment. "I guess it sounds kinda... peaceful."

"It was," I said, smiling. "And they didn't even miss Wi-Fi."

"They lived off of onions and bread," Zaya said. "Sounds like something a Telkkeppyana would say," I said. "They lived a beautiful simple life based on faith, family, and service."

"Speaking of Telkeppyane, plural," said Mr. Yatooma. "If you want to learn more, you have to read Father Bazzi's several books about the topic. He's our number one expert."

"Who is he?" Mary asked.

"He's someone every Chaldean should know," I said. "He left the town of Tel Keepe in 1972 to study in Rome, but the town never left his heart. Aside from writing books about it, he has taught Aramaic at Cuyamaca College from 1989 until he recently retired."

"Wow, that's a long time," Lola said.

"He carries with him the most precious souvenirs in a box that stays by his bedside wherever he lives," I said.

"What does the box have in it?" Zaya asked.

"A little stone from the Rock over the Well on the Hill, one from Mar Gorgis Monastery, and another from the Western Gate of Nineveh's ruins," I said. "There's also some dirt and a piece of old pottery from the same place. And it has soil from his family home, some paper money from different places, and two stamps—one with a harp from the ancient city of Ur, and the other with the Winged Bull of Nimrud."

"How do you know all this?" someone asked.

"I've read his books and even interviewed him," I said. "He's a wonderful, loving, and wise man who is completely dedicated to preserving the Chaldean heritage."

A silence of admiration absorbed those words.

"Now, let's get back to the topic of bread," I said, "I think our friend over there has been patiently waiting for us to appreciate her work."

The group turned back to the tableau of the Chaldean woman, her hands still rolling dough as if she'd been listening to every word. For a moment, the room was quiet, the weight of Tel Keppe's history settling over us.

"Let's keep going," I said softly. "There are more villages, more stories, and more whispers waiting for us."

CHAPTER 2

The Heart Beneath the Mountain

"This exhibit is dedicated to Alqosh," I said.

"Like that song?" someone asked.

"Yes, like that song," I replied, and before I knew it, the children started singing:

Alqosh, ya matha d'zona

Alqosh, ta kollan 3ona

"This is outrageous!" said Helen just as I said, "This is adorable."

She huffed and added, "Well, at least translate the words for those of us who don't understand Chaldean."

And so, with the help of Mr. Yatooma, we translated the song:

Alqosh, village of ancient times

Alqosh, a beacon for us all

Alqosh, Alqosh, a necklace of roses above our hearts

Alqosh, Alqosh, a necklace of roses above our hearts.

The dancing continued even after the singing stopped. The adults watched with joy until I realized time was running out. I had to bring everyone back to the exhibits.

"This is a replica of Rabban Hormiz Monastery," I said.

"Whoa," Zaya said as he took it all in. "This looks fancy."

The walls were painted with sweeping landscapes of jagged mountains, rolling hills, and stone houses perched along steep cliffs. The monastery replica stood at the center, carved into the cliffside with intricate details. Arched windows, worn stone walls, and tiny staircases made it look almost alive.

"Is that the place we talked about before?" Zaya asked, pointing at the monastery.

"It is," I said. "Glad you were paying attention. Remember? We talked about how it was built in the 600s—over 1,400 years ago!"

"Oh, yeah!" Zaya said, snapping his fingers. "That's the one where the monks lived. Didn't you say it's still there?"

"It is," I replied. "And not just Rabban Hormiz. Alqosh has many important sites, but this monastery is one of the most famous."

Lola squinted at the replica. "How did they even get up there?"

"Did they climb it like Spider-Man?" John asked.

The group laughed, and I shook my head. "No webs involved, John. But they did climb. The monastery is high up in the mountains to protect it from invaders. It's not easy to reach, even today."

Mr. Yatooma stepped forward, ready to join the conversation. "And that's not all, kids. Alqosh is more than just a place for monks. It's a village with a long history of protecting people. When other villages like Tel Keppe were attacked, Chaldeans fled to Alqosh for safety."

"Why wasn't Alqosh attacked?" Mary asked, her pencil poised over her notebook.

"Great question," Mr. Yatooma said, pacing slightly as if he were in a courtroom. "Alqosh was spared because of its location. The mountains and cliffs made it difficult for invaders to reach, and the people there knew how to defend their village. Even when ISIS attacked nearby areas, they never touched Alqosh. That's why it's still standing today—untouched and full of history."

"So, it's like the ultimate hideout," John said, nodding.

"Guess you could say that," Mr. Yatooma said, pointing at him. "A fortress of faith and resilience."

Mary scribbled something in her notebook, then looked up. "What else?"

"Well, there's a tomb there, too," he said.

"Of a prophet," I added.

"A prophet?" Lola asked, wide-eyed.

"Yes," I said. "The tomb of the Prophet Nahum is in Alqosh. He's a prophet from the Bible, and his tomb has been preserved for centuries. It's a sacred site for both Christians and Jews."

Zaya raised his hand. "So, like, an *actual* prophet is buried there? Not just a statue or something?"

"An actual prophet," I confirmed.

"Whoa," Zaya said. "That's cool. Is it, like, hidden or in a cave or—"

Before he could finish, Lola chimed in. "Or maybe it's in a secret underground hideout with booby traps, like in the movies!"

"Lola, you have quite an imagination!" I said. "But no, no secret hideouts, Lola, but the tomb is a special place. People from all over the world visit it."

John leaned in closer to the replica, his eyes narrowing. "So, are there any secret tunnels here?" He knocked lightly on the false walls. "Anyone there? Anyone?"

"John, stop it!" said his mother, Helen.

Mr. Yatooma chuckled. "If there are, they're still a secret. But I wouldn't be surprised if the monks had a few hidden paths. They were very resourceful."

"Resourceful and brave," I added. "The people of

Alqosh have always been protectors—of their faith, their history, and their community."

"What about now?" Mary asked. "Do people still live there?"

"Yes," I said. "Today, Alqosh is a peaceful place where many Chaldeans still live. It's also a popular destination for visitors. You can walk through its streets, visit the monastery, and see the vineyards and valleys stretching out for miles."

Lola sighed dreamily. "I'd live there. I'd wake up every morning, look out at the mountains, and write poetry or something."

"Or open a spaceship café," Mary teased.

"Wake up on the rooftop in the summer to the sound of roosters cock-a-doodle-dooing and flies stretched across your face," Zaya added.

Everyone grimaced. "Gross," said some of the children, while others chimed in with, "Disgusting!"

"Hey, that's what the old people told me," Zaya said defensively.

"I wouldn't mind that one bit," John said with a smile.

As the children laughed and carried on, caught up in the humor, I gently brought them back to the topic. "Alqosh is a reminder of our history and resilience. Even when other villages were destroyed, Alqosh stood strong. It's a symbol of hope."

Zaya nodded thoughtfully. "So, it's like the superhero of villages."

"Exactly," I said. "And its story is one of the reasons why we're here today—to remember and celebrate the strength of our people."

The group fell quiet for a moment, their eyes lingering on the replica of Rabban Hormiz and the mountain landscapes. Even John, who usually had something funny to say, seemed lost in thought.

As we gathered around the miniature model of Mosul's landmarks, I pointed to a beautiful structure. "This," I said, "is the famous Mar Gorgis Church and Seminary. It's not just a church—it was also a seminary where priests trained. Families would gather here for worship and community events."

"Oh, absolutely!" Mr. Yatooma said, his face lighting up with nostalgia. "My family and I used to rent rooms at the seminary for a night or two. It was like our little vacation spot. We'd pack up the car, load up the *julyatha*—hand-woven rungs—and head out to the farm nearby."

"What did you do there?" Mary asked, curious. "Pray all weekend? Read ancient scrolls?"

"Ha! No, Mary, we weren't that serious," Mr. Yatooma said, laughing. "We'd park the car by the farm, lay out a blanket, and barbecue. Oh, and dance! Lots of dancing. My dad would bring out the *doumbek*, and before you knew it, everyone was doing the *chobi*! Even the chickens near the grill looked like they wanted to join in."

Lola raised an eyebrow. "You danced *with* the chickens?"

"No, no!" Mr. Yatooma said, shaking his head. "But if you saw how they flapped around the barbecue grill, you'd think so!"

"So, basically," Zaya said, grinning, "you turned the seminary into a party zone. Did the priests ever join in?"

"Not that I remember," Mr. Yatooma said, "but I swear I saw one priest peek out the window once. He was tapping his foot to the beat. I think he wanted to join us, but, you know, holy dignity and all that."

I shook my head, smiling. "Mr. Yatooma, I think you've just given these kids the wrong impression of seminary life."

"No," Mary said seriously, "I think he's given us the *right* impression of how to have fun. Can we go there now?"

"Yeah!" Lola added. "I want to dance with the barbecue chickens!"

I chuckled. "Well, the seminary isn't exactly a weekend rental anymore. But you can still visit the church, learn its history, and maybe have a picnic nearby. Just leave the chickens alone."

"Noted," Zaya said, pretending to jot something down. "No chickens. But can we bring the doumbek? I want to see if I can make the priests tap their feet!"

"That's the spirit, Zaya," Mr. Yatooma said, clapping him on the back. "You'd fit right in with my family back then."

"Alright, alright," I said, waving them toward the next exhibit. "Let's move on before this turns into a doumbek full-blown dance party!"

Everyone laughed as they followed me. Zaya mimicked a drumbeat on an invisible, and Lola spun around, pretending to dance with imaginary chickens. It was moments like these that made sharing history so much fun.

Finally, Mr. Yatooma clapped his hands together. "Alright, kids! Let's keep moving. There's more to see, and I'm sure Ms. Weam has a few more surprises waiting for us."

The children snapped out of their reverie, their chatter and laughter filling the gallery once more. Alqosh had shared its whispers, and now, it was time to hear the next.

CHAPTER 3

Echoes of the Homeland

The children's laughter and chatter echoed as we moved into the next exhibit. If Tel Keppe was the cradle of heritage and Alqosh the heart of the mountain, this section was the soul of the villages—small communities scattered across the Nineveh Plain and beyond, each with its own story, traditions, and resilience.

"This exhibit is dedicated to the other villages of our ancestors," I said, gesturing toward the room filled with artifacts. "Places like Batnaya, Karamlish, Araden, Bartella, Bakhdida, Tesqopa, Baqofa, Amadia, and many others. Much like Tel Keppe and Alqosh, these places hold centuries of history and culture within them."

Mary looked up from her notebook, where she had jotted down most of what I said. "So, did all Chaldeans come from these villages?"

"Most Chaldeans today trace their roots to

Telkaif, but many to other small villages in the northern Nineveh Plain," I explained.

"Guess for the Chaldeans, there's no need for 23andMe," said Helen.

"Sorry?" I said.

"You know, to figure out where they came from," Helen continued, smirking. "Their history is already carved into stone tablets somewhere, isn't it?"

Zaya stroked his chin thoughtfully. "Yeah, but it'd still be cool to get a DNA test back and it just says, 'Congratulations, you're 100 percent Chaldean.'"

"'Now go learn how to make kebabs,'" added John, grinning.

The group burst into laughter.

"Or kubba," said Lola, giggling as Mary joined in, tossing out more food names like taghrathid pusra.

"Now, now, children," I said, reeling them back in. "Let's focus on the tour. And remember, Chaldeans' roots didn't start in the villages. As I've shared in previous galleries, the Chaldeans originally lived in southern Mesopotamia."

"Yeah, you explained it, but it's still confusing," Lola said, rolling her eyes.

"What's confusing?" Mr. Yatooma asked.

"Well, I heard we only became Chaldean in 1553..."

"Not true!" Mr. Yatooma said. "That's a myth."

The group leaned in, curious. Zaya even stopped fiddling with his shoelace.

"Let's go back to the Council of Florence in 1444—over a hundred years before 1553," Mr. Yatooma said. "At that council, Archbishop Timothy identified as the leader of the Chaldeans, a group with their own language, culture, and faith. The council even mentioned the 'Chaldean tongue,' their Aramaic dialect. This shows the Chaldeans were already recognized as a distinct people long before 1553."

"So the Vatican didn't make up the Chaldean title?" Lola asked.

"Not at all," Mr. Yatooma said. "Timothy's union in 1445 was about faith—it recognized the Chaldeans in Cyprus as part of the Catholic Church. But it didn't create a new patriarchate."

"What about 1553?" Mary asked.

"That was different," he explained. "By then, the Church of the East was struggling with corrupt leadership. Yohannan Sulaqa went to Rome for authority, and the Pope made him the first 'Patriarch of the Chaldeans.' This created a new patriarchate in Mesopotamia, marking the formal establishment of the Chaldean Catholic Church."

"So Timothy's union was spiritual, and Sulaqa's was structural?" Zaya asked.

"Right," Mr. Yatooma said. "You see, when times got tough—like during the Muslim conquests or Mongol invasions—many Chaldeans migrated north."

"That sounds rough," John said.

"Oh, it was," Mr. Yatooma chimed in, stepping forward with a spark in his voice. "But here's the thing—out of all that chaos, these villages were born. And get this—they're all different, but they've got a lot in common, too. Most of them were way out in the middle of nowhere, so they became super self-reliant. Each one ended up with its own little personality."

"Like Tel Keppe?" Mary asked, scribbling in her notebook.

"Exactly!" I said. "Tel Keppe was the largest Chaldean town in the region. As I mentioned earlier, it wasn't just a village—it was actually the center of a whole district in the Nineveh Governorate, with many surrounding towns and villages."

"And get this," Mr. Yatooma added enthusiastically. "Tel Keppe was a lookout for the whole area. They kept an eye out for trouble and helped protect the surrounding towns."

"I thought Alqosh did that," Zaya asked, leaning in.

"They both did until ISIS destroyed Telkaif,"

Mr. Yatooma said. "Now, Alqosh had other special traits. Over time, it turned into a cultural hotspot. Generations of calligraphers and artists came from there. Everywhere you go, there's history and creativity."

"Remember that, despite their differences," I said, "villages were united by a shared history and religion, and by a common language, Aramaic."

The children's eyes darted to the displays, captivated by the items that brought these villages to life. Cooking utensils, farming tools, and hand-embroidered tablecloths were arranged alongside jewelry, rifles, and colorful scarves.

"What's that?" Zaya asked, pointing at a long-handled Turkish coffee pot.

"That's what people used to make coffee," I said. "It's called a *rakwe*. Coffee was a big part of social life in the villages. Families and neighbors would gather to share stories over a cup."

Lola leaned closer to examine a massive round bowl. "And this?"

"That's a *tahshut*," I explained. "It was used for kneading dough or preparing large meals for the family. Like in most cultures, food was for nourishment and a way to bring people together."

As the children studied the artifacts, I added,

"Did you know that the first recipes were found in ancient Mesopotamia?"

"Really?" Mary asked, her eyes lighting up. "Where are those tablets?"

"The originals are at the Peabody Museum," I said, pointing at an enclosed display, "but here we have replicas."

The children crowded closer, staring at the replicas with admiration. "Whoa," Zaya whispered. "So, people were writing down recipes thousands of years ago?"

"They were," I said with a smile. "And these recipes weren't that much different than our foods today. They included things like stews, bread, and even beer."

"Beer?" someone asked, surprised.

"Remember the ancient gallery we visited earlier?" Mr. Yatooma jumped in. "We talked about the first recipe for beer. Remember Ninkasi?"

"Who?" several of them asked in unison, their faces scrunched with confusion.

"Ninkasi!" he said, almost reprimanding. "She was the goddess of beer in ancient Mesopotamia. They even wrote a hymn to her that stood as a recipe for brewing beer."

"Ohhh, yes, I remember her," Mary said, flipping

through her notebook. "I wrote that down. Ninkasi… goddess of beer. Got it!"

Mr. Yatooma gave her an approving nod. "Good! See? History can be pretty fun when you get to learn about gods, recipes, and a little beer brewing."

The children giggled, and Zaya said, "All this talk about recipes is making me hungry."

"Just don't let the beer recipe make you tipsy," Helen said, rolling her eyes.

Mr. Yatooma cleared his throat, shooting her a glance that said, *Really?*—ironic, considering she was usually the one scolding him. Without missing a beat, he gestured toward another display. "Alright, moving on. These tools show just how self-sufficient these villages were. People farmed the land, made their own crafts, and protected their homes with grit and ingenuity. And check this out—maps of farmland and old land transaction documents. Agriculture wasn't just a job; it was their lifeline."

The children wandered from one display to the next, marveling at the craftsmanship of the baskets, sifters, and slingshots. A few boys gathered around a collection of knives and rifles.

"Whoa, were these used in battles?" John asked.

"For hunting and protection," Mr. Yatooma clarified. "Villagers had to defend themselves, especially during times of war or invasion."

Lola pointed at a doll dressed in intricate clothing. "What about this? Did kids play with these?"

"Yes," I said with a smile. "Each village had its own unique style of clothing, even for dolls. Look at these scarves and *kutchma* headdresses—they reflect the traditions of places like Karamlish and Tesqopa."

I led them to a display of benches and cushions. "Homes were simple but full of warmth," I said, running my hand over the worn wood. "Families would gather on the floor, spreading a blanket to eat meals together or tell stories late into the night. These jars here were used to store food like *turshi*—pickled vegetables made to last through the seasons. And these woven fans… they brought relief during the sweltering summer heat."

Zaya picked up a pipe from one of the displays and touched its intricate design. "Did people make these by hand?"

"They did," I replied. "Crafting pipes like these was an art."

"Smoking pipes was common in many villages, especially for men," Mr. Yatooma said. "It was often a social activity, a way to share stories and bond after a long day of work."

"Occasionally," I said, smiling, "women like Maria Theresa Asmar would pick one up too."

The children giggled as they imagined life in the villages, their curiosity growing as they listened.

"These villages were more than just places to live," I continued. "Each one held a piece of Chaldean history, culture, and resilience. Take Bakhdida, for example. It has many names—Qaraqosh, Karakosh, Al-Hamdaniya—but it has always been the heart of Iraq's Christian community."

"What happened to it during the wars?" Mary asked in a quiet voice.

I took a deep breath, the weight of history filling the room. "In 2014, ISIS invaded Bakhdida," I said. "The entire population of 60,000 people was forced to flee in just a few days. They were given a cruel choice—convert to Islam or be killed. The town was left in ruins. Churches, homes, and schools were burned. The fields that once fed so many were destroyed."

The children's faces fell, their eyes wide with disbelief.

"But in 2016, Bakhdida was liberated," I continued, my voice steady. "The people returned—not all of them, but enough to begin rebuilding their lives. Even now, the town is still recovering. Only about half its residents have returned, and the scars of what happened are still visible." I paused, then added softly, "In 2023, a fire at a wedding hall killed over 120 people. It was another tragedy for a community that has endured so much."

"What was Bakhdida like before all this?" Lola asked, her voice filled with longing.

"Before the wars, Bakhdida was full of life," I said, my tone brightening slightly. "It was known for its agriculture, with over 190 poultry farms feeding much of northern Iraq. Its churches, like the magnificent Al-Tahira Cathedral, were the pride of the community. Education was another cornerstone—Bakhdida's schools and teachers were among the best in the Nineveh Plain. Even today, the University of Hamdaniya continues that legacy, preparing doctors, engineers, and leaders for the future."

The children listened silently, their expressions a mix of sadness and admiration.

"And then there's Bartella," I said. "It's another historic Christian town, known for its Syriac Orthodox heritage and its beautiful churches, like Mar Shmoni. But Bartella has faced significant demographic changes. Many Christian families have left, and the town is now shared with the Shabak community. Still, those who remain continue to protect their traditions and their faith."

"Now," I said, motioning to the next exhibit, "let's talk about life in the mountains, like in Araden and Amadia."

The children followed me quietly, their footsteps producing a soft echo against the floor.

"Araden is surrounded by breathtaking natural beauty," I said. "Its lush orchards and forests were lovingly tended by skilled farmers. The villagers were also known for their woodworking, creating intricate carvings that adorned homes and churches."

"Amadia?" John asked pointing to a name on the map. "It sounds like a girl's name, like Amanda."

"Ah, Amadia," I said with a hint of awe. "One of the oldest towns in the region, perched high in the mountains. Its history stretches back thousands of years. It was once a regional center, and its stone fortresses tell stories of ancient battles and enduring resilience."

The children whispered among themselves, their eyes lingering on the artifacts that seemed to breathe life into the stories.

"Do you want to tell them about Sharafiya?" asked Mr. Yatooma.

"Oh, yes, of course!" I said. "My cousin and her family live there. It's the smallest village I've ever heard of, with only about twenty families."

Mary's face lit up. "Oh, how lovely! I'd love to live in a tiny village like that."

Mr. Yatooma's expression grew serious. "Before

ISIS attacked, Sharafiya had about 400 families," he said quietly.

The children sighed, their sadness clear.

I added gently, "But the good news is that the Church of St. George was restored, and baptisms resumed in January 2018."

The children cheered. Even Helen joined in.

"Each of these villages has its own story," I said, my voice filled with emotion. "They've faced unimaginable hardships but have always found a way to endure. Whether through faith, education, or the strength of their communities, they carry the legacy of resilience."

The children clapped in celebration. Mr. Yatooma clapped his hands to gather their attention. "Alright, kids! Let's not linger too long. Ms. Weam has so much more to show us."

As we left the exhibit behind, I smiled to myself. The villages had spoken, their stories woven into the fabric of our identity. And now, they'd passed their whispers on to a new generation.

CHAPTER 4

Dancing with Tradition

The group moved toward the interactive displays, and I stopped in front of one labeled *Chaldean Weddings.*

"This is one of my favorite exhibits," I said, gesturing to the display. "Check out these dolls dressed in traditional Chaldean wedding outfits—they're miniature works of art!"

The dolls stood proudly, each one a vibrant display of color and detail. Among them, the bride and groom drew the most attention: the bride wore a glittering pink robe with gold designs, a matching *kutchma* crown, and layers of gold jewelry that sparkled from head to toe. Beside her, the groom stood tall in a long black robe, a crisp white *dishdasha*, and a white-and-black checkered headdress.

"They seem ready to step off the display and join a wedding celebration," said Helen.

"They do look eager to dance the *chobia,* don't they?" I joked.

"Oh, oh, can we dance with them?" Zaya asked and the children extended their hands to join fingers and form circles. Mr. Yatooma and I stopped them.

"Let's pay attention to Ms. Weam," he said.

"Alright, has everyone been to a Chaldean wedding?" I asked.

More than half the group raised their hands.

"Well, those who have, you'll know what I'm talking about. And those who haven't—make sure your Chaldean friends invite you to one at some point in your life. You honestly don't want to miss this!"

"Can you invite us to your wedding, Ms. Weam?" one of the children asked.

"Well, I would, but I'm already married," I said, eyeing Mr. Yatooma, who smiled. "But with Michigan having the largest population of Chaldeans in the world, with over 200,000 Chaldeans, you're bound to find someone to invite you!"

The children giggled and chit-chatted with excitement. I pressed the display, and the sounds of the *zerna* and *tabul* filled the room. On the screen, a grand wedding entrance unfolded: the bride and groom were surrounded by family and friends, clapping and cheering as they danced their way into the banquet hall.

"Wow!" Mary said.

"This is what makes Chaldean weddings so unforgettable," I explained. "The music, the dancing, the joy—it's all a celebration of love and community."

"What are we hearing now?" asked Helen.

"These instruments are the same ones used in the olden days," I said, "when weddings were celebrated in the streets."

"Right in the street?" someone said.

"Yes," I said. " People would hand out chocolates—or even shots of *arak*—as the bride and groom were paraded through the village."

"Greeks did the same," said Helen, proudly.

"And Italians too," I said. "Has anyone ever seen *The Godfather*?"

The kids looked at me blankly, while the adults nodded knowingly.

"Wow, I guess I'm older than I thought," I said with a laugh. "But for those who know it, there's a scene where Michael Corleone and his bride are paraded through the town in Sicily, surrounded by villagers singing and celebrating. That's what weddings in the Christian villages of Iraq looked like."

"The bride had a lot of walking to do," said Lola.

"Well, she rode a donkey," Mr. Yatooma said.

The children broke into a loud laughter.

"What's funny?" he asked. "Back then, a donkey was like today's limousine."

The laughter grew louder, so I cut in. "It's amazing how much cultures have in common."

I pointed to the video on the screen, now showing a modern Chaldean wedding and zooming in on the bride's dress. "Notice the bride is wearing white? That's not a Middle Eastern tradition. It started with Queen Victoria in 1840. Before that, brides wore colorful dresses—or even black ones—to avoid stains!"

"Black wedding dresses?" Lola asked in surprise.

"That's strange," said Helen.

"Some wore red, others green," I said. "It was practical. But after Queen Victoria's trend-setting moment, people worldwide adopted the white wedding dress. Just another example of cultures borrowing from each other."

I gestured to the video again. "Here, you'll also notice a crown placed over the bride and groom. That's not originally our tradition—it's Greek."

Helen's face lit up. "Really?"

"Yes! They borrowed it from your ancestors, Helen," I said. "It's a beautiful tradition that symbolizes the unity of the couple, and it's one that Chaldean weddings have adopted. But the language of the ceremony the priest is using? That's Chaldean. Brides and grooms today have the option of having their ceremony in Chaldean, Arabic, or English, which is yet another way cultures borrow from each other, adopt, and grow."

"Did you see the awesome Assyrian and Indian wedding?" someone asked.

"No, I didn't," I said.

"It was all over social media!" someone else said.

"Yeah, we saw it," Lola and Mary said.

The children chatted excitedly about the beautiful blending of traditions.

At this point, Helen raised her hand. "Can I ask a sensitive question, if I may?" she asked carefully.

"Of course," I encouraged.

"Why are some Chaldeans offended when called Arabs?"

The question hung in the air for a moment. I could see the kids' faces shift—some looked curious, while others, like Zaya, frowned slightly.

"Well," I began, "it has to do with the traumatic memories associated with that word. When Arab Muslims invaded Mesopotamia in the seventh century, they brought Islam and imposed their rule. Non-Muslims—like the Chaldeans—were forced to either convert to Islam or pay a tax, because they were considered *dhimmis*—nonbelievers and second-class citizens. Many who couldn't pay the tax were persecuted or fled. These events created a lot of pain and left scars that haven't fully healed, especially since as recently as 2014, ISIS attacked and destroyed many of our ancestral villages."

The room was silent, the gravity of the history settling over the group.

"The trauma hasn't had a chance to fully heal," I continued, "because minorities still feel unprotected and aren't given the rights they deserve."

"Oh," said Helen.

"That said," I elaborated, "we can't deny that in the 1,400 years the country has been Arab, we've adopted many traditions. It's natural. And there are so many beautiful traditions from the Arab community that, like ours, go back thousands of years—such as their deep sense of hospitality."

Helen nodded thoughtfully. "Are you offended when someone calls you an Arab?"

I smiled softly. "Well, no, but then again, I'm not someone who easily gets offended."

The kids laughed, breaking the tension.

"Those who are offended, as I mentioned, still feel hurt from the past," I said. "Some want to protect their ancient name, which, as we've discussed, people have tried to erase. But unless we were born outside of Iraq or before 1921, when Britain changed the name of Mesopotamia to Iraq… well, we were born in an Arab country. Our citizenship states that."

I gestured to the group. "Think about it—all who

were born there speak Arabic and read and write it fluently, whereas few know how to read and write Chaldean. We eat Middle Eastern foods, listen and dance to Arabic songs, watch Arabic soap operas, and pay big bucks to go see Kathem Al Sahir."

"Who's that?" a kid asked, wrinkling his nose.

I gasped theatrically. "That's the most famous Iraqi singer! Everyone loves him. But guess what— he's an Arab who sings Arabic songs!"

The kids snickered, and Helen smiled, visibly impressed by the nuanced explanation.

"Not all Arabs are Muslims, and not all Muslims are Arabs," I added. "Arabs have their own ancient history, rich with contributions to art, science, and culture. And many Muslims today don't agree with the oppressive practices of the past. It's a complex topic, rooted in history, but also evolving with time."

"Bravo, Ms. Weam," said Mr. Yatooma. "We love everything you just said, don't we, class?"

A chorus of loud and soft "Yeses!" filled the room, a sound that felt like the most beautiful song to my ears.

I bowed playfully and concluded, "There's a lot to cover about this subject, which we'll explore more in the Genocide Gallery."

Just then, a melody burst from the interactive display as one of the kids pressed a button, curious to see what it would do. The lively rhythm of a traditional Chaldean wedding song filled the room, and the group perked up. Zaya began tapping his foot, and Lola swayed slightly to the beat.

With a grin, one of the boys grabbed a tissue from his pocket, held it high, and started moving to the music.

"Oh, so you guys want to do the *debka*?" I asked, laughing.

"I thought it's called *chobia*," someone said.

"It all depends whether you're speaking in Arabic or Chaldean," I explained, "which proves my earlier point."

Zaya held out his hand to Mary. "Either way, *yalla!* Let's do it!"

Mary linked her hand with Zaya's, and one by one, the children joined hands, forming a line. They moved in unison, stepping and stomping to the beat of the zerna and tabul. Even Mr. Yatooma joined in, but his movements were off, and he was clearly struggling to keep up.

"Come on, Mr. Yatooma!" Zaya shouted. "Left foot, right foot!"

As Mr. Yatooma attempted to get his footsteps right, the line grew longer, snaking around the display. The kids picked up their pace to the beat of the drums, their feet flying and their laughter echoing through the gallery.

After several minutes, Helen raised her hand, pretending to be out of breath. "Okay, okay, this was fun but also exhausting. Can we have a snack break?"

I clapped my hands lightly to gather their attention, but no one heard me or Helen as the rhythmic echoes of the zerna and tabul followed us, dancing our way to the next exhibit.

CHAPTER 5

The Ink of Our Ancestors

As the music of the zerna and tabul faded and we left behind the joyful energy of the wedding exhibit, I turned to the group. "Now that we've danced the chobia and celebrated love, let's talk about another thing that brings people together—learning."

"Learning?!" Zaya groaned, dragging his feet dramatically. "We just had so much fun. Why do we have to talk about school?"

"Yeah, I agree!" another kid chimed in, while someone else shouted, "Let's take a vote!"

"Ah, but wait!" I said, raising a finger. "Schools in the villages were unique, as you'll soon find out. Some of the greatest writers and educators in Chaldean history came from these tiny villages."

That got their attention.

We stopped in front of an exhibit featuring old books, quills, and a replica of a classroom. A small wooden desk with carvings etched into it sat next to a massive chalkboard, where someone had written

Shlama alukhun! (Peace be upon you!) in beautiful Chaldean script.

"Long, long ago," I began, "schools were rare in Iraq, especially in the villages. Churches and mosques stepped in to educate people before the government began opening public schools. In Tel Keppe, for example, the church played a huge role in teaching children. Did you know the first person to write a book there was Patriarch Yousif II Al Maroof? He was born in 1667 and was educated by some of the best teachers of his time. And here's something amazing—by 1855, people had already written about studying in a Catholic school in Tel Keppe."

Mary squinted at the display. "You mean schools in the villages go back that far?"

"They do!" I said. "And they weren't just for boys. Girls received an education thanks to the Dominican Sisters of St. Catherine of Siena, who opened a convent in Tel Keppe in 1900. They taught girls Chaldean, Arabic, and French. Imagine being a girl in the nineteenth century and learning three languages!"

"Wow," Helen said, her voice tinged with admiration.

"My grandma only spoke Chaldean," Lola said. "And she never went to school."

"Well, not everyone went to school," I said. "A lot

of boys and girls helped their families on the farm or in the home. Girls often got married when they were very young and didn't get the chance to get an education."

"That's sad," Mary said, looking at her notebook as if to say, *I can never imagine what it would be like to not read or write.*

"It was, but those women were no less smart, Mary," I said. "They had a wisdom many intellectuals will never understand."

Mary smiled, evidently feeling better.

"That sounds like my grandma!" said Lola. "She was the smartest woman I know!"

"My mother too," I said. "But back then, education was about more than just reading and writing. It was about gaining life experience, preserving culture, language, and tradition."

"Yes!" Lola cheered, startling everyone. We turned to look at her in surprise.

"When schools like Al-Irfan opened in 1922, that was such a big deal," I said. "They taught everything from math to Turkish to French—and later, English. And they made learning accessible to everyone, no matter how remote the village."

Mr. Yatooma's voice brightened as he said, "And let's not forget the poets and authors who came from Tel Keppe. Did you know there was a female poet named Haneh Nwetha Dallo? Lola and Mary, you'll love this! She couldn't read or write, yet she composed some of the most beautiful religious poems, which are still preserved in the Dominican library in Mosul. Now that's pure talent!"

"Yes!" Mary and Lola cheered in unison.

"Wait, she couldn't read or write?" Zaya asked, his jaw dropping.

"That's right," I said. "Her poems were so powerful that people called her a prophet. And then, of course, there's Maria Theresa Asmar, who traveled the world and wrote *Memoirs of a Babylonian Princess.*"

"I can't wait to read her memoir one day," Mary said, her eyes distant.

"Oh, you'll love it," I said. "She documented her incredible journey, meeting royalty and sharing her life as a Chaldean woman in the nineteenth century. But I'll warn you—it's quite long."

"How long?" Mary asked, intrigued.

"Well, it's two volumes, about 700 pages total," I replied.

"Wow!" Mary said, her excitement faltering slightly. "That's a lot of reading."

"That's why I wrote an abridged version," I reassured her. "It's about 300 pages—much easier to manage."

"Now *that* I can handle," Mary said with a grin, and Lola nodded in agreement.

"It's inspiring," I added, "because her story captures the challenges and triumphs of being a strong woman in a male-dominated world. It's a message that still resonates today."

I led them to another display featuring old classroom photographs. "Did you know that until 1951, kids had to travel all the way to Mosul for middle school and high school? Imagine walking miles every day just to get an education!"

"That reminds me of a movie I saw called *On the Way to School*," Zaya said suddenly. "It's about kids from all over the world walking hours to school. One kid even rode a donkey through the mountains!"

"That's a great comparison, Zaya," I said.

"That sounds like an interesting movie," Mr. Yatooma chimed in. "We should show it in class so some of you complainers start appreciating school—and me!"

"Mr. Yatooma, we *do* appreciate you," said John with a wide smile.

Zaya smacked John on the back in playful support, and Mr. Yatooma gave them a mock stern look.

"The Chaldean community in Baghdad eventually helped open middle and high schools in Tel Keppe," I continued. "By 1959, these schools were thriving. And by the 1990s, you couldn't find a college or institute in Iraq without at least one student from Tel Keppe."

"That's incredible," Mary said, gazing at the photos.

"It is," I agreed. "Chaldeans knew that education would give their kids the tools to build something bigger than themselves. And look at the results. People from these villages became famous authors, poets, journalists, professors, and even government leaders. Some of their works are still used in schools today."

"Like who?" Zaya asked, clearly intrigued despite himself.

"Well, Dr. Naim Yousif Sarafa is a great example. He eventually earned his Ph.D. in education from Wayne State University in Detroit and became Iraq's Deputy Minister of Education. He wrote 23 books on teaching methods!"

"Whoa," Zaya said, genuinely impressed.

"And then there's Mrs. Mariam Narme," I added. "She was Iraq's first female journalist. In 1937, she even published her own newspaper called *Al-Arab Girl*. She wrote over 100 essays and received a medal from the Pope for her charity work."

"Okay, that's pretty cool," Mary admitted.

The kids wandered around the exhibit, marveling

at the old books and artifacts. Mary pointed to a giant book on display. "What's this?" she asked.

"That," I said with a dramatic pause, "is one of Tel Keppe's prized possessions. It's a religious book written in 1586. It's so big and heavy, one person can't carry it alone."

"Why would they make a book that huge?" Zaya asked, his eyes wide.

"Because knowledge is heavy," I said with a wink.

The group burst into laughter, and I clapped my hands. "Alright, who's ready to learn more about the incredible people who made all this possible?"

The kids cheered, their excitement renewed as we moved on to the next part of the exhibit.

CHAPTER 6

Fashion and Folklore

As we moved away from the exhibit on education, I glanced at the group. "Now that we've explored how knowledge shaped Tel Keppe, let's take a closer look at something just as telling—how people expressed their identity through what they wore and how they sang."

The kids followed me to a display featuring mannequins dressed in traditional Chaldean clothing. The vibrant colors of the women's dresses shimmered under the lights, and the intricate silver belts seemed to tell their own stories. Nearby, another case held gold and silver jewelry, some adorned with precious stones, while a brightly colored scarf rested delicately on top of the display.

"Wow, is that real gold?" Zaya asked, pointing to a necklace.

"It is," I said. "In the old days, gold and silver jewelry were a part of a woman's dowry and a reflection of her family's wealth and status."

"Why is everything so long?" Lola asked, gesturing toward the flowing dresses.

"Back then, modesty was very important, especially when going to church," I said. "Women wore long dresses that reached their feet, often with brightly colored scarves to cover their hair. Men, on the other hand, wore long robes paired with a head covering. The clothing wasn't so much about fashion as it symbolized tradition and respect for their faith."

Helen leaned closer to the display, examining the silver belt. "Did they wear this every day?"

"Not always," I replied. "These belts were often reserved for special occasions—weddings, feasts, or church celebrations. But even their everyday clothing was practical and reflected their connection to the land. They used fabrics that were durable and lightweight, perfect for the hot climate."

Beside the clothing display was a small section dedicated to the art of singing and poetry. A recording played softly in the background—a woman's mournful voice chanting an elegy.

"Do you hear that?" I asked, gesturing toward the sound.

"It's kind of sad," Mary said, her eyes tearing.

"That's because it's an elegy," I explained. "Years ago, life in Tel Keppe was very hard. People worked long hours in the fields, and many couldn't read or write. Singing was something they did often, not only on special occasions like weddings or church celebrations. But when someone passed away, women expressed their grief through a form of wailing called an elegy."

"What's she saying?" Zaya asked.

"It's a poem about loss and sorrow," I said and pressed a button on the screen that showed the translation of the elegy.

Oh my beloved, taken by the wind,
Where now do your footsteps tread?
The earth that cradles you is silent,
But my heart, oh, it wails instead.

In Tel Keppe's fields, we played as children,
Under the sun's warm, golden light.
Now the Lord watch over your rest,
While your family weeps through the endless night.

Your laughter once filled these walls,
A melody sweeter than the church bells' toll.
Now only echoes remain in the stones,
And a prayer burns deep in our soul.

I noticed tears in some of the children's eyes.

"These women turned their cries and pain into poetry," I said. "They'd chant about the person who had died, remembering their life and the impact they had on others."

Lola crossed her arms. "My grandma used to sing something like that at funerals. She said it was to honor the person."

"Isn't that something special?" I asked. "Even though these women didn't have formal education, they had an incredible ability to create poetry on the spot. They turned their emotions into art."

"When they did this," Mr. Yatooma added, his voice soft, "it wasn't just words—it was their soul speaking. The rawness, the truth, the love they poured into those chants could move people in ways no written literature ever could. It was alive, it was spoken from the heart, and it was shared in the sacred moment of grief. That's what made it unforgettable."

"They were not pretentious, were they?" Helen asked tenderly, as if wishing that people nowadays were less pretentious.

"No, they were not pretentious," I said. "They wore their hearts on their sleeves, as the saying goes."

"What about happy songs?" Zaya asked.

Before I could answer, Helen pointed to a large plaque on the wall. "What's this?"

We walked over to the display, which was surrounded by candles and flowers. At the top, the
words *"In Memory of the Lost"* were engraved. Below
it was a list of names.

"This," I said, "is a memorial to those who lost
their lives in the flood of Tel Keppe. Have any of you
heard of it?"

Some nodded while others shook their head.

"On April 1, 1949, a devastating disaster struck
the village," I began. "A flood came with terrifying
speed and force, catching everyone off guard. Forty-
two girls, one infant, and one man lost their lives.
The children were in school, and their teacher, thinking it would be safer, kept them in the classroom.
Tragically, the classroom was on a lower level, almost like a sunken space, and when the water came
rushing in, it rose too fast. The smaller ones couldn't
climb to safety in time. That day, the school became
a tomb, and it remains one of the darkest chapters
in Tel Keppe's history."

The kids leaned closer, reading the names on
the plaque.

One of them broke the silence. "My great aunt
was five when it happened. She survived by running
outside. My grandpa told us about it. He was one of
the people who went to help, and he found one of

the girls who had drowned and brought her back to the village."

I had my own story to share. "My cousin's sister and her aunt were little—three and five. When they pulled them out of the water, they were holding hands and... dead."

The kids gasped. The room fell silent, the sound of the elegy in the background seeming to grow louder in the quiet space.

"These stories," I continued, "are why the elegies meant so much. They were a way for people to grieve, to honor those they lost, and to make sure their memories would never fade."

The recording of the elegy continued softly as the group lingered by the plaque, their curiosity replaced by quiet reverence.

"So, what about happy songs?" Zaya repeated his earlier question, breaking the silence.

"Oh, there were happy songs too," I said, grateful for the chance to lighten the mood. I pressed the button on the screen to stop the elegies. "Aside from the ones at weddings that we talked about earlier, they sang to preserve stories, pass down traditions, and bring people together."

The kids wandered around the exhibit, marveling at the intricate clothing and listening to the recordings of songs and poems. I pointed to a small plaque beside a beautifully embroidered dress.

"Did you know," I said, "that every bit of embroidery on these dresses was done by hand? Women would spend weeks, even months, creating these masterpieces. Each pattern told a story—whether it was about their family, their village, or their faith."

"That must've taken forever," Mary said.

"No, not forever, but a long time," I said. "But it also brought people together. Women would often gather in groups to sew, sharing stories and building bonds while they worked. And just like the songs and poems, these clothes became a way to preserve their identity."

As we moved toward the next section, Zaya stopped in front of a mannequin of a man wearing a scarf and layers of traditional clothes. "Do you think they'd let me wear this to school?" he asked.

Mr. Yatooma laughed. "I think you'd probably get some funny looks, Zaya. But who knows? Maybe you'd start a new trend."

The group laughed, and I gestured toward the next display. "Alright, let's keep moving. Next up: how the people of Tel Keppe used their knowledge of nature to heal their communities."

The kids followed eagerly, their excitement carrying us into the next chapter of Tel Keppe's story.

CHAPTER 7

Healing Hands and Herbal Remedies

We left behind the vibrant colors and songs of the previous exhibit and stepped into a quieter, earthier space. The air smelled faintly of lavender and mint, and the display cases were filled with dried herbs, tiny glass bottles, and old tools that looked like they belonged in a medieval workshop.

"This," I said, gesturing to the room, "is where we learn about medicine in Tel Keppe. Long before doctors and pharmacies became common, villagers relied on nature—and each other—to heal."

Zaya squinted at a jar filled with what looked like dried leaves. "So, they didn't have doctors?"

"Not in the way we think of them today," I replied. "Most people couldn't afford to see a doctor, and even if they could, there weren't many around. So, they turned to what they had: plants, herbs, and the wisdom passed down from their ancestors. Midwives, barbers, and elders were the community's healers."

Mary looked up from her notes. "Ms. Weam, didn't you say you come from a family of healers?"

"Yes, I do," I said. "Thank you for remembering."

"Who did you say were healers?" Lola asked.

"Well, my father, who was the head of the accounting department at Baghdad Railway Station, was a bonesetter—for no charge. His sister, Hassina, was a midwife. His grandfather was a healer, and his grandmother too."

"That's a lot of family doctors," said Mary.

"It is," I said. "And it's something I'm very proud of. They were healers and problem solvers who cared deeply about their community."

"Excuse me," a boy interrupted, raising his hand. "Did you say barbers?"

"Uh, well." I gestured toward a display of tools that looked alarmingly sharp. "The barber wasn't just responsible for cutting hair—he was also the village dentist."

The fear in the children's eyes was both amusing and understandable.

"You're saying the same guy who gave haircuts *also* pulled teeth?" Zaya asked, wide-eyed.

"Yes. If someone had a toothache, they'd go to the barber," I explained. "He kept a set of tools in his shop and would pull the tooth free of charge.

But since they weren't exactly trained dentists, there was a catch."

"What kind of catch?" Helen asked, leaning forward with curiosity.

"Well…" I hesitated, unsure how to phrase it delicately. I glanced at Mr. Yatooma, who jumped in without missing a beat.

"Sometimes," he said, "they'd pull the wrong tooth."

The group erupted into a mixture of gasps and laughter. Zaya rubbed his jaw as if feeling the phantom pain. "Yeah, I think I'll stick to modern dentists," he said.

"A very wise decision," Mr. Yatooma replied, patting his back.

I gestured to another display filled with dried herbs and small mortar and pestle sets. "But it wasn't all barbers and guesswork. The people of Tel Keppe were incredibly resourceful when it came to healing. They knew which plants could treat different illnesses. For example, if someone had an eye infection, they'd soak a cloth in water mixed with *khabuz*— that's a type of dough paste—and place it on the eye. If something got stuck in the eye, they'd put a drop of oil in it and, believe it or not, someone would use the tip of their tongue to remove it."

"That's so gross!" Lola cried, covering her eyes.

"Not really," one kid said. "This could solve problems."

Lola looked at him quizzically.

"My parents couldn't find the tweezers once," he said. "They had this huge fight. If they knew about the alternatives, maybe they'd just lick it out and save the drama."

"This is making me queasy," Helen muttered, taking a step back. "When is it going to end?"

"We're almost done," I said, starting to feel nauseous myself. "They made do with what they had. For gum disease, they used a natural herb called *blue khusa* or a material called *sheb*. And if someone had a serious toothache, they'd chew on cloves to numb the pain."

Helen wrinkled her nose. "But what about bigger problems? Like broken bones?"

"Well," I said, "for injuries like that, they'd rely on midwives and nurses."

"Or your dad," Mary interjected, and I gave her a wink of acknowledgement.

"Midwives, like my aunt, weren't just there to deliver babies," I said. "They were the go-to experts for a lot of health issues. They used splints made of wood and cloth for broken bones and treated headaches, stomachaches, and earaches with herbal teas and poultices."

"What the heck is that?" John asked.

"John, no swearing," Helen scolded, crossing her arms.

"That's not a swear word!" John protested. He turned to Mr. Yatooma. "Is it?"

"Ah, well…" Mr. Yatooma stammered, clearly unsure how to navigate this linguistic minefield.

I jumped in to rescue him. "A poultice," I said, "is like a paste or mash made from crushed herbs, plants, or even bread. They'd spread it on a cloth and press it against the skin to draw out infections or reduce swelling."

"Wait," Zaya said, his face lighting up with mock horror. "So, you're telling me they slapped a soggy bread sandwich on people to make them better?"

"Pretty much," I said, laughing. "But it worked! For example, if someone had a headache, they might use a poultice made of crushed mint leaves. Or if someone had a swollen ankle, they'd use one made of crushed onions to help ease the pain."

"Onions?" Lola groaned. "Gross. They'd smell like onion soup!"

"Better than a swollen ankle," I said. "And sometimes they'd even use mashed garlic for infections."

"*Tuma*?" Zaya cried, using the Chaldean word for garlic. "Yuk!"

"Imagine walking around smelling like a kitchen

of chicken, roast, dolma!" said Mr. Yatooma, joining in.

"Now I'm hungry," Zaya said, rubbing his stomach.

I pointed to a small bottle in the corner of the display to refocus them. "And this," I said, "is one of the most interesting remedies. Do you know what it's for?"

"Uh… perfume?" Lola guessed, leaning closer.

"Not quite," I said. "It's oil mixed with herbs, used to treat ear infections. They'd warm it slightly and pour a drop into the infected ear."

"Okay, that's less gross," Zaya admitted. "But I'm still thinking about the soggy bread thing."

The group laughed, but Mary tilted her head thoughtfully. "Did it work, though?"

"Most of the time," I said. "But not always. People trusted these remedies because they were passed down through generations. And while they often worked wonders, there were times when nothing could be done. Living conditions in Tel Keppe weren't always sanitary. People lived with farm animals, dealt with polluted water, and had to fend off poisonous insects. These things made it hard to stay healthy."

The kids fell silent for a moment, taking this in.

Then Lola asked, "What about babies? How did they take care of them?"

"Great question," I said. "Midwives were especially skilled at caring for newborns and mothers. They used herbal remedies to help with pain and recovery after childbirth. And if a baby got sick, they'd use teas made from chamomile or mint to soothe them."

Helen pointed to a large book on display. "What's this?"

"That's a collection of natural remedies written by one of the village elders," I said. "It's full of recipes for treating everything from colds to skin infections. These books were like gold to the community because they held the secrets to survival." I paused, then added, "Of course, there were more serious illnesses that they couldn't cure."

"Like what?" Mary asked.

"Oh, many things," I said softly. "For instance, my oldest brother, George. He died of diphtheria when he was a toddler because they didn't have medicine for it back then. Had it happened now, they could have cured him in a synch!"

The room grew quiet for a moment before Mary said gently, "I'm sorry about your brother."

"Thank you, Mary. That was a long time ago,

and although I never met him, I know his loss devastated my parents."

Zaya stared at the book again, then turned to me. "Do you think any of this stuff would work today?"

"Some of it, definitely," I said. "In fact, a lot of modern medicine is inspired by traditional remedies. But we're lucky to have doctors and hospitals now. Back then, people had to rely on nature—and hope for the best."

The moved on, the image of onion poultices and garlic remedies lingering in their minds—and noses.

"Alright," I said, leading them toward the next section. "Let's leave the world of herbs and barbers behind. Next up: how village people celebrated life together, through holidays and holy days."

CHAPTER 8

Feasts, Fasts, and Fires

The next exhibit seemed to hum with life. Church bells chimed softly in the background. The air carried the faint, smoky scent of frankincense. Displays glowed with photographs of celebrations and religious relics. A table was set with plates of pacha and kuleche, as if prepared for a feast.

"Now," I said, turning to the group, "let's talk about something that brought everyone in Tel Keppe together: holidays and holy days."

Zaya sniffed the air. "What's that smell? It smells… spicy."

"That's probably the pacha," I said, pointing to the table display. "It's a traditional dish made from lamb, stuffed with rice and spices. And it was a big part of Christmas celebrations."

Lola wrinkled her nose. "We still eat that, but some of stuff in there gross me out, like lamb tongues."

The children made ooh sounds while a few of

the boys said, "Yum" and laughed. Helen rolled her eyes and looked she was about to puke. "Please, no more talk about tongues," she said.

Mr. Yatooma cleared his throat and clapped his hands. "Boys and girls, let's listen up," he commanded.

"After Midnight Mass," I said, "everyone would come home to eat pacha. Some families didn't even sleep. They'd stay up all night until Mass ended at three in the morning and then feasted together. And of course, they'd also eat kuleche—cookies stuffed with dates and nuts."

"Now that sounds better," Zaya said, eyeing the fake kuleche on the display.

Voices saying "Oh, I love kuleche" echoed through the gallery.

"Just like here and in other parts of the world," I continued, "Christmas was a time for visiting family and friends to congratulate each other. People wore their best clothes and shared tea and pastries."

Helen raised her hand. "What about New Year's? Did they celebrate that too?"

"They did," I said. "Families would stay up all night again, eating and celebrating the last hours of the year. And after New Year's, they celebrated Epiphany, the Baptism of Jesus. That's when two men would sit in front of the church with a large bowl of holy water, placing a cross in it. As people passed by, they kissed the cross as a sign of blessing."

"That's so beautiful," Mary said softly, clearly imagining the scene.

"Yeah, pretty cool," said Lola.

I pointed to another section of the display, where candles surrounded a small model of a whale. "And here we have Baoutha, the three-day feast commemorating the story of Jonah and the Whale."

A few students nodded, recalling our earlier discussion in the Faith and Church Gallery.

"Thank you for being such attentive listeners," I said. "As you remember, Baoutha lasted three days, during which people fasted, prayed, and attended church every morning until noon. Some didn't eat anything at all for the entire three days, while others gave up meat and dairy."

"That sounds really hard," Lola said.

"It was," I said. "But at the end of the fast, there was a special treat: *Halawat Khedir Elias*, a sweet dessert made just for that occasion."

Helen nodded. "A celebration after the fast. I like that."

"Me too," I said. "And every season had its own rhythm of fasting and feasting. Lent was another big part of life in Tel Keppe. People fasted for fifty days, eating only vegetables and sesame butter with bread.

Each Sunday during Lent was devoted to a particular saint, and people celebrated at small shrines dedicated to them."

I gestured to another display featuring palm branches and tiny crosses. "And of course, there was Palm Sunday, which was a really exciting time. The priest, deacons, and children would carry palms in a procession, blessing homes as they walked."

"Yo, yo, yo! Get this!" Mr. Yatooma jumped in, clapping his hands to make sure he had everyone's attention. The kids turned to him immediately. "Palm Sunday isn't just about walking around with a leaf in your hand, alright? There's a *story* here—a good one. You ready?"

"Ready!" the kids chorused, leaning closer.

"So, check this out." He pointed to the palm branches in the display. "These bad boys? They go *way* back. Like, *ancient Mesopotamia* back. That's where our people come from—the cradle of civilization, where they were farming, building ziggurats, and making up the first written language. Remember all that from the ancient gallery?"

They nodded.

"And guess what?" he asked. "The palm tree was a big deal back then, too. It wasn't just a tree; it was like the king of trees. It meant life, prosperity, and good vibes."

"Good vibes?" Zaya asked, laughing.

"Yeah, good vibes!" Mr. Yatooma said, pretending to wave a palm branch like a wand. "Back then, they thought palms had some serious magic. You see, Mesopotamia was all about rivers. No rivers, no food. No food, no people. The palm tree was like a gift from the gods because it grew in the middle of all that. So naturally, they associated it with life and blessings. And get this—they even tied it to their gods. Ishtar, the goddess of fertility and love? Remember her?"

The children nodded.

"Palm tree," said Mr. Yatooma. "Shamash, the sun god? Palm tree. It's all connected!"

The kids were hooked now, giggling as Mr. Yatooma mimed waving to the gods.

"Now, fast forward a couple thousand years," he said, pretending to spin an imaginary clock. "When Christianity showed up in Mesopotamia, they didn't just ditch all that cool symbolism. Oh no. They kept it, but they gave it a new twist. The palm branch became a sign of victory—Jesus' victory over sin and death. That's why on Palm Sunday, we wave them around like there's no tomorrow. It's like saying, 'Hey, Jesus! You're the greatest of all time!'"

The kids burst out laughing.

"Every Palm Sunday, when you hold that branch,

think about this," Mr. Yatooma said, leaning in conspiratorially. "You're holding history! That branch connects you to ancient Mesopotamia, to Jesus, to your great-great-great-grandparents, and to every Palm Sunday that's ever happened. How cool is that?"

"Super cool," Zaya said, his voice filled with awe.

Mary lifted her pen midair. "So, when we're waving palms, we're basically doing what people have done for thousands of years?"

"That's right!" Mr. Yatooma said, pointing at her like she'd just won a game show. "You're keeping the tradition alive. It's like you're part of this epic story that goes way, way back."

I smiled, watching the kids' faces light up. Mr. Yatooma had a way of making everyone feel connected to the past, a way that was fun and meaningful.

"Thank you, Mr. Yatooma, for sharing this fascinating history about the palm," I said. "Now, going back to Palm Sunday. Families would give gifts to the priests, deacons, and children carrying palm for blessing their homes."

"What kind of gifts?" Zaya asked.

"Usually food or tokens of appreciation," I said. "But the real celebration came during Holy Week. People were busy cleaning their homes, sewing new clothes, and baking kuleche for Easter. On Good Friday, there would be a procession to remember the death of Jesus, and on Easter Sunday, people went to Midnight Mass. When the priest declared that Jesus had risen, everyone clapped and cheered."

"That sounds fun," Mary said, smiling up from her notebook.

"It was," I said. "For Easter, they had special customs too, like boiling and dyeing eggs for children."

"My grandma said they mostly colored the eggs brown," Lola added.

"That's true," I said. "They didn't use store-bought dyes like we do. They'd boil onion skins to make the water brown and then dip the eggs in it."

"Cool!" the kids said in unison.

"The week after Easter, second graders would receive their First Holy Communion," I continued, "dressing in white to mark the occasion. It was a big deal for the whole community."

Zaya pointed to a photo of boys and girls splashing each other with water. "What's going on here?"

"That's Ascension Day," I said, laughing. "Forty days after Easter, boys and girls would splash water on each other. If you were walking outside, you were fair game!"

"That's my type of game," said John, grinning.

"It was definitely fun," I said. "But if you think that's wild, wait until you hear about the Feast of the Holy Cross. On September 14th, the men would carry a huge steel tub on their heads—filled with burning manure or dried grass."

"Wait—*burning*?" Zaya asked, his eyes wide.

"Burning," I confirmed. "They'd use a pillow to protect their heads and go house to house, saying things like, 'Imad's underwear is on fire!' Then they'd pass the tub to the next man."

The kids erupted in laughter.

"Why manure, though?" Lola asked, cringing.

"It burns slowly," I said. "Perfect for keeping the fire going."

"And nobody got fried?" John asked.

"Nope," I said. "They kept it moving, like a flaming relay race."

Zaya smirked. "Do you think they ever stopped to grill hot dogs on it? Maybe roast marshmallows?"

"Or make s'mores!" Mary added, giggling.

"Yeah, nothing says faith and community like, 'Pass me the marshmallow stick!'" John chimed in, pretending to hold out a skewer.

The group burst into laughter again.

"It was an honor to carry the fire," I said, smiling. "It showed strength and faith."

"Or maybe it was just their way of weeding out the faint of heart," said Helen. "Nothing says leadership like balancing the weight a large flaming tub of manure on your head."

The kids roared with laughter.

"Well, maybe," I said, chuckling. As we moved toward the next exhibit, I added, "They were definitely full of spirit, and we'll see how they carried that spirit to their next stage of life in another chapter."

CHAPTER 9

Journeys of the Heart

As we entered the next exhibit, a soft train whistle sounded, accompanied by footsteps on gravel. Black-and-white photos lined the walls, showing people with suitcases, boarding boats, and standing with their families in distant cities. A world map on the far wall, dotted with pins, marked where the people of Tel Keppe, Alqosh, and nearby villages had settled.

"This chapter," I began, "is about journeys—heartbreaking yet hopeful. Let's explore why people left northern Iraq and what they found in new lands."

Mary pointed to a photo of a family by a cart piled high with belongings. "Why did they leave?"

"There were many reasons," I said, gesturing to the timeline on the wall. "The first wave of migration started in the nineteenth century. Some left because of economic struggles. Life in Tel Keppe was hard—people were poor, and after World War I, many were starving. Others left because of political instability, especially under the Ottoman Empire. They were looking for safety, for opportunities, for a better life."

I paused in front of a portrait of Ms. Maria Therese Asmar. Dressed in elegant clothing, she looked every bit the world traveler she was.

"Take Ms. Maria Therese Asmar," I said. "Born in 1806, she was one of the first pioneers to leave Tel Keppe. After her father died, she moved to Baghdad and later traveled to Lebanon, Italy, France, and England. She devoted herself to educating girls in the Middle East."

"What an amazing woman!" Mary said.

"She was," I agreed. "Queen Victoria of England believed in her so much that she sponsored her memoir."

"A genius," Mary said, her pen hovering over her paper as she imagined the story.

"What happened to her?" Lola asked.

"She passed away in Paris in 1870," I said. "Before she died, she left $5,000 to remodel the Saint Peter and Saint Paul Church in Tel Keppe. She wanted to be buried there, and her wish was granted."

"I want to learn more about her," Mary said.

"We'll be sharing more of her story in the Genocide Gallery," I replied.

Zaya raised his hand. "So, did everyone go to Europe?"

"Not at all," I said, leading the group to the map. "People from Tel Keppe spread out all over the world. Some went to Baghdad and other cities in Iraq, like Mosul, Basra, and Kirkuk. Others went to Turkey, Mexico, Canada, and the United States. The reasons for leaving were often the same, but the journeys were very different."

I pointed to a section of the map marked "Baghdad." "The first people from Tel Keppe to move to Baghdad were Yousif Pattah and his sons in 1875. Others followed, and by 1967, there were 14,000 people from Tel Keppe living in Baghdad. Most of them worked in shops or as professionals—doctors, engineers, and teachers."

"Ms. Weam, weren't you born in Baghdad?" one of the children asked.

"Yes, I was. Once my father and mother married, they lived in Baghdad, so all their children were born there."

Zaya squinted at the map. "What about this part—Mexico?"

"That's a fascinating story," I said. "The first person to move to Mexico was Mr. Petu Koryoka in 1838. Later, others followed, like Mr. Jajoo Haji. Some of them married Mexican women and stayed there, while others returned to Iraq or moved on to the United States. By 1967, there were about fifty Chaldean families living in Mexico."

"If you want to learn about the Chaldeans in Mexico," said Mr. Yatooma, "you should read Dr. Ulises Casab Rueda's book *Ixtepec-Telkef: The Iraqi Christians in Mexico*."

"How do you spell that?" Mary asked.

"Which, the author or the book title?" he asked.

"Both," she said.

After Mr. Yatooma spelled the words for Mary, Helen pointed at the section marked "Detroit." "What about here?"

"Ah, Detroit," I said with a smile. "That's where many people from Tel Keppe ended up, especially in the early twentieth century. Most of them worked in grocery stores. One of the first pioneers to settle in Michigan was Mr. Zia Acho, who arrived in 1913 after living in Canada. He started by selling food from a vending cart, and as more people arrived, they opened small stores."

"Was it hard for them?" Mary asked.

"Very hard," I said. "They didn't speak the language, had little money, and didn't know anyone. Some even got lost on the way. One man had a letter with him indicating he was supposed to go to Michigan, but when he arrived in New York City, he didn't know where to go. A translator pinned a note to his back that said 'Detroit,' and he was put on the right train."

The kids laughed at the thought, and Zaya said, "At least they figured it out."

"They did," I said. "And they helped each other. Whenever someone new arrived, those already settled would offer help, whether it was finding a job, learning the language, or just navigating a new city."

I pointed to a photo of a family waving goodbye at a train station. "But leaving wasn't easy. When someone left Tel Keppe, it was heartbreaking. Families would cry because they thought they'd never see each other again. Back then, traveling was dangerous and expensive. It wasn't like hopping on a plane today."

"What about the people who stayed?" Helen asked.

"They kept the traditions alive," I said. "And so did those who left. Even in Detroit, you'll find Chaldeans celebrating Christmas with pacha and kuleche, just like they did in Tel Keppe. They built churches, opened schools, and passed down their language and culture to the next generation."

As we moved to the final display, I gestured to a quote etched into the wall: *'No matter how far we go, Tel Keppe is always in our hearts.'* Similar quotes were made about the other villages such as Alqosh, Batnayeh, and others.

"That's what made the village people so special," I said. "They adapted to new places, built new lives, but they never forgot where they came from. They carried their traditions, their faith, and their sense of community with them, turning every new land into a little piece of Tel Keppe."

The group lingered for a moment, taking it all in. Then Mary said softly, "I guess they didn't really leave Tel Keppe behind, did they?"

"No," I said with a smile. "They brought it with them, wherever they went."

CHAPTER 10

A Window into the Past

The kids practically sprinted into the final exhibit, their excitement reaching a fever pitch. In the center of the room stood an elegant window, framed in dark wood and polished to a shine. Beneath it, a brass plaque read: *Through this window, the past comes alive.*

"What's this?" Zaya asked, craning his neck to peer through the glass.

"Careful, don't push!" I said, laughing as the kids jostled for position.

"It's called Pepper's Ghost," I explained. "When you look through the window, it activates scenes from daily life in the villages. But only one person can watch at a time!"

"Dibs!" Zaya shouted, squeezing his way to the front.

"No cutting!" Mary cried, trying to elbow her way in.

"Guys, stop shoving!" Helen said, rolling her eyes but sticking her head in the fray all the same.

Finally, everyone calmed down enough to take turns. Zaya leaned in first, resting his forehead against the wooden frame.

The window flickered to life.

Scene One: Dinner on the Floor

The glass showed a small, cozy room with a family of four sitting cross-legged on the floor. A mother, father, and two children—one boy, one girl—gathered around a large platter of food. Steam rose from bowls of stew, and the soft crackle of bread being torn echoed faintly.

"They're eating on the floor?" Zaya said, his voice full of wonder.

"That's how most families ate back then," I said. "They didn't have dining tables like we do now. Sitting on the floor was a way of connecting—not just with each other but with the earth, their home."

In the scene, the mother handed a piece of bread to her son while the father poured water from a clay jug. The family spoke animatedly, laughing and gesturing as they shared their meal.

"That looks like fun," Lola said as Zaya stepped aside. "My turn!"

John tried to squeeze in, but another boy piped

up in a mock-parental tone, "*Qaleit kalba, meewit bewatha?*"

Both Mr. Yatooma and I froze, exchanging wide-eyed glances. "Oh no," I said, shaking my head. "Let's not go there."

"What does that mean?" Helen asked.

"You don't want to know," I said quickly.

"Actually, I do want to know," Helen said.

The boy who said it grinned mischievously, clearly proud of himself for using an expression he'd heard from an elder who'd said, "You dog, what are you doing?" But thankfully, the kids weren't fazed. I dodged Helen's question by pointing out scene two of Pepper's Ghost.

Scene Two: Preparing for School

Lola leaned in, and the scene shifted. Now the mother was sitting on a woven mat, carefully braiding her daughter's hair. The little girl squirmed, clearly impatient, but the mother held her head steady, her fingers working quickly and expertly.

"See how they're getting ready for school?" I asked. "The mother would make sure her daughter looked presentable before heading off to learn."

"Did they have backpacks?" Mary asked.

"Not like the ones you know," I said. "They

carried books and supplies in cloth bundles or small schoolbags."

In the glass, the mother tied the braid with a bright ribbon and kissed her daughter's forehead. The little girl grabbed a small bag and darted out of the room with utter excitement.

"That's sweet," Lola said, stepping back.

Scene Three: A Father and Son's Lesson

Helen leaned in, and the scene changed again. Now the father and son were outside in a dusty yard. The father knelt beside his son, showing him how to use a slingshot. The boy watched intently as his father placed a small rock into the sling and pulled it back. With a sharp snap, the rock sailed through the air, hitting a tin can perched on a fence.

"Cool!" Zaya said, craning his neck to see over Helen's shoulder.

"Back then, slingshots were more than toys," I explained. "They were tools for hunting small game or scaring off birds from the fields. Fathers taught their sons how to use them responsibly."

The boy in the scene took the slingshot, his hands trembling slightly as he pulled the sling back. He missed on his first try, but the father patted his shoulder encouragingly. On his second attempt, the can toppled over, and the boy beamed with pride.

Scene Four: Making Kubba

Mary stepped up next, and the scene shifted indoors. In the kitchen, the mother's hands were coated in a mixture of rice and meat as she shaped kubba into perfect ovals. Her mother-in-law sat beside her, while the daughter tried to help, struggling to get the shape right.

"Back then, families lived in multi-generational homes," I said. "Everyone shared the work, which made things easier."

"Bet there were a lot of fights too," Helen said with a smirk.

"Well, can't argue there," I replied. "There's even a folk song from Tel Keppe about a feud between a mother-in-law and daughter-in-law. It got so bad, the man caught in the middle ran away from home like a madman."

The adults laughed.

"You can read the whole song in one of Father Bazzi's books," I added. "But thankfully, there were a lot more peaceful stories."

"That looks delicious," Mary said.

"It is," I replied. "Making kubba was often a family activity. Mothers taught their daughters recipes passed down through generations, each family adding their own twist."

In the scene, the mother smiled patiently as her

daughter's lumpy kubba fell apart. She showed her how to press the mixture firmly, cupping her hands just right. This time, it held together, and the daughter clapped her hands in triumph.

Scene Five: Nighttime Stories and Lullabies

The last scene began as the group crowded around for one final look. The family was gathered around a small heater, the mother pouring tea into tiny glass cups. The father leaned back, telling a story with grand gestures as the children listened, their eyes wide.

"What are they talking about?" Zaya asked.

"Probably a story about their ancestors," I said. "Families often told tales to teach lessons or share history."

The scene dimmed slightly as the family finished their tea and began laying blankets on the floor. The father and mother tucked the children in, pulling the covers tightly around them. The mother sat beside them, her voice soft as she began to sing:

Oh Tel Keppe, you are honey in my mouth
Oh land of my father and mother
Your name I bear within me
Your soil I mix with my blood

Her voice was gentle, almost a whisper, yet it carried the weight of generations.

In Chaldean:
Tel Keppe dousha b-kimmee
Ya athra d-babi w-yimmee
Shimmakh bta-ninne immee
Uprakh bgolinne b-dimmee

As the mother's song faded, the scene dissolved into darkness. The group stood in silence for a moment, the weight of the past settling on their shoulders.

"That was beautiful," Mary said softly.

"It really was," Zaya agreed, for once not cracking a joke.

I smiled. "That's the magic of village life."

As the kids slowly made their way out of the exhibit, I lingered by the window for a moment, gazing into the now-empty glass. For just a second, I thought I could still hear the mother's lullaby, a whisper from a time long gone but never forgotten.

The End

YOUR TURN TO EXPLORE!

1. **Village Storyteller**
   - Ask your family members to share a favorite story about their hometown.
   - Write your own short story inspired by life in a village.

2. **Map Your Roots**
   - Create a map of your family's village or town. Include landmarks like schools, churches, or markets.
   - Mark where your family home is (or was) on the map.
   - Add a legend to explain any special features or symbols on your map.

3. **Village Time Capsule**
   - Collect items or photos that represent your family's village or hometown.
   - Write a letter to future generations explaining why these items are important.
   - Seal your collection in a box to create a "time capsule" for your family.

4. Traditions Keeper

- Interview someone in your family about a tradition they remember from their childhood.
- Recreate or adapt that tradition with your own twist (e.g., cooking a traditional dish or celebrating a festival).
- Write about how the tradition makes you feel and why it's important to keep it alive.

5. Village Voices

- Record a conversation with a family member about their experiences growing up in a village or small town.
- Write down three lessons or values they learned from their community.
- Share these lessons in a drawing, poem, or short video.

6. Cultural Connections

- Research a festival or holiday celebrated in your family's village or culture.
- Compare it to a holiday you celebrate now—what's similar and what's different?

7. **Museum of Memories**
   - Design a mini-exhibit about your family's village. Include photos, drawings, or objects.
   - Write short descriptions for each item, just like in a museum.
   - Invite friends or family to view your exhibit and share their own stories.

CONTINUE THE JOURNEY

Want to explore more stories about our ancient heritage and modern adventures? Here are some books you might enjoy by Weam Namou:

- The Magical Museum Series
- Little Baghdad
- Pomegranate (also available as a movie)
- Mesopotamian Goddesses
- Iraqi American Series: The Lives of the Artists

You can find these books on Amazon or visit www.weamnamou.com to discover more stories!

Other Great Books About Chaldean History and Culture:

Visit your local library or bookstore to discover more wonderful books about Chaldean history and culture! You can also ask your teachers and family members to help you find age-appropriate books about our rich heritage.

ABOUT ME, YOUR MUSEUM GUIDE AND CHALDEAN STORYTELLER!

I was born in Baghdad, Iraq as a Chaldean—we're Christian Catholics also known as Neo-Babylonians, and yes, we still speak Aramaic, the language Jesus spoke! When I was your age, just ten years old, my family and I moved to Michigan in the United States. Did you know Michigan has the largest population of Chaldeans in the whole world?

People call me the Chaldean Storyteller because I've been writing stories for almost as long as I can remember. Stories help us understand who we are and where we came from, and I've written nearly two dozen books so far! I've also made two movies that have won over forty awards. Sometimes

I still can't believe that the little girl who moved from Baghdad grew up to tell stories that people all around the world want to hear.

I speak three languages—English, Arabic, and Aramaic—and I love to travel and learn about different cultures. I studied writing in college and even learned poetry in a beautiful city called Prague! When I'm not writing or producing films, I'm spending time with my two beautiful children, my husband, and our lovable dog who always makes us laugh.

In 2019, I began an exciting journey when I became the executive director of the Chaldean Cultural Center. That's where you'll find the world's first and only Chaldean Museum—the very one you've just visited through this book.

As a writer and filmmaker, I feel so honored to create stories that touch people's hearts and to share our incredible history with young people like you. Every time I tell someone about our past, I'm not just teaching them history—I'm helping them discover pieces of themselves they never knew existed.

www.ingramcontent.com/pod-product-compliance
Lightning Source LLC
Chambersburg PA
CBHW070941250626
47159CB00009B/3341